First Facts®

Positively Pets

Caring for Your
Horse

by Erin Monahan

Consultant:
Jennifer Zablotny, DVM
Member, American Veterinary Medical Association

Capstone
press®

Mankato, Minnesota

First Facts is published by Capstone Press,
151 Good Counsel Drive, P.O. Box 669, Mankato, Minnesota 56002.
www.capstonepress.com

Library of Congress Cataloging-in-Publication Data
Monahan, Erin, 1977–
    Caring for your horse/by Erin Monahan.
    p. cm. — (First facts. Positively pets)
    Summary: "Describes caring for a horse, including supplies needed, feeding, cleaning, health,
safety, and aging" — Provided by publisher.
    Includes bibliographical references and index.
    ISBN-13: 978-1-4296-1256-2 (hardcover)
    ISBN-10: 1-4296-1256-8 (hardcover)
    1. Horses — Juvenile literature. I. Title. II. Series.
SF302.M64 2008
636.1'083 — dc22
                                               2007030369

Editorial Credits

Gillia Olson, editor; Bobbi J. Wyss, set designer; Kyle Grenz, book designer and illustrator;
    Kelly Garvin, photo researcher/photo stylist

Photo Credits

All photos Capstone Press/Karon Dubke, except page 20, Shutterstock/Winthrop Brookhouse

Capstone Press thanks Rock King, owner of Sun Up Construction, Madison Lake, Minnesota,
    Mary Frantenberg, owner of Stony Ridge Tack and Stable, Abby Viessman of Mankato,
    Minnesota, and their accommodating staff for use of their fine facilities and beautiful horses.

1 2 3 4 5 6 13 12 11 10 09 08

Table of Contents

Do You Want a Horse?

With speed and grace, horses gallop through fields. Maybe you have ridden one of these big, gentle animals. Maybe you've petted its soft nose.

Do you dream of owning a horse? A horse is a lot of responsibility. Horse owners say the hard work is worth it.

For your first horse, get an older, experienced animal. Have someone who knows about horses help you pick one out.

Your Horse on the Farm

Horses need to live on a farm. They need fields for galloping and a stable for shelter. City people can own a horse by paying to **board** it at someone's farm.

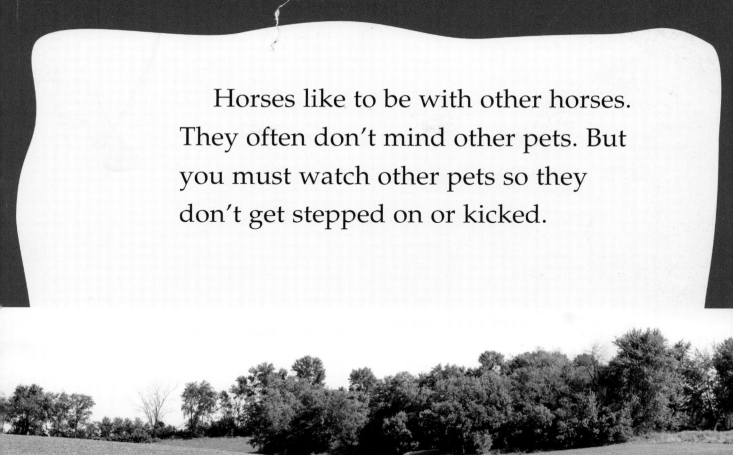

Horses like to be with other horses. They often don't mind other pets. But you must watch other pets so they don't get stepped on or kicked.

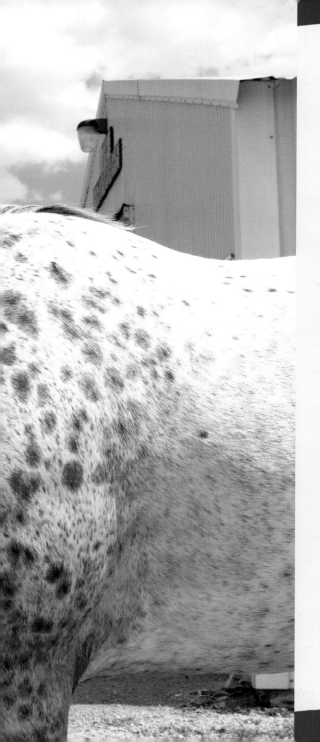

Supplies to Buy

You'll need brushes, a **halter**, and lead rope. The brushes will keep the horse's coat clean. The halter and lead will help you control the horse.

If the horse will live on your farm, you will need more supplies. Buy grain, hay, and buckets for food and water from a farm store. If you board, fees often include these things.

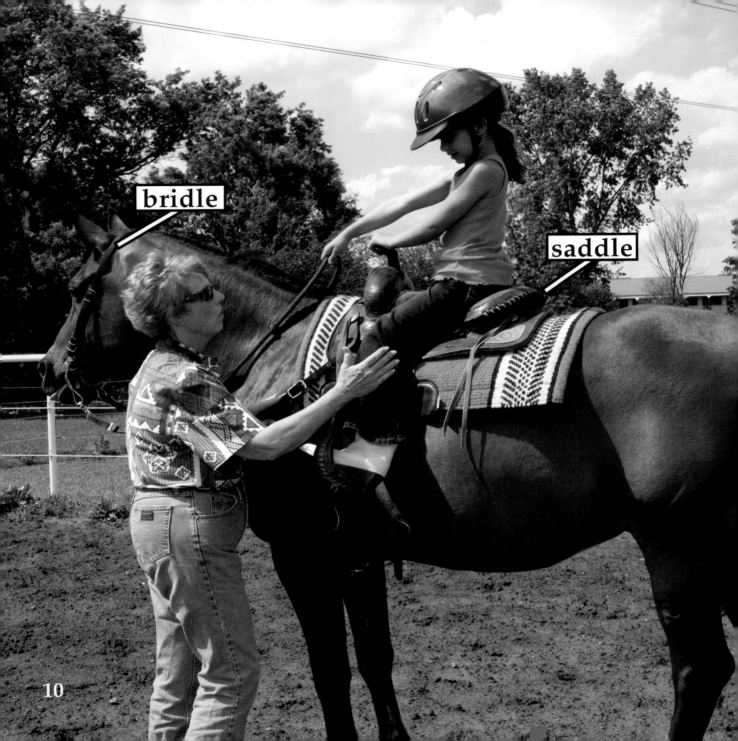

bridle

saddle

10

Riding Needs

To ride your horse, you will need a **saddle** and a **bridle**. Riding boots and a helmet will help keep you safe.

Riding lessons are very important. Take lessons from a riding teacher. It's the best and safest way to learn to ride.

Make sure to pick a saddle that fits both me and you. The best way to see if a saddle fits is to try it on my back.

Feeding Time

Make sure your horse has fresh water at all times. Twice a day, horses need to be fed hay and grain. The amount of food a horse needs depends on its age and activity level. Ask your **veterinarian** how much to feed your horse.

Carrots and apples are my favorite treats. Just don't feed me too many, or I might get sick.

Brushing and Cleaning

Horses like to roll around in the dirt. Brush your horse often to help keep it clean. Also keep your horse's hooves free of rocks and dirt clumps.

Stall cleaning is a smelly but important part of horse care. Every day, scoop out dirty hay and poop. If you board, stall cleaning is often included in the fee.

A Healthy Horse

A veterinarian should see your horse at least once a year. Horses need shots and a check up. Vets also help sick or hurt horses.

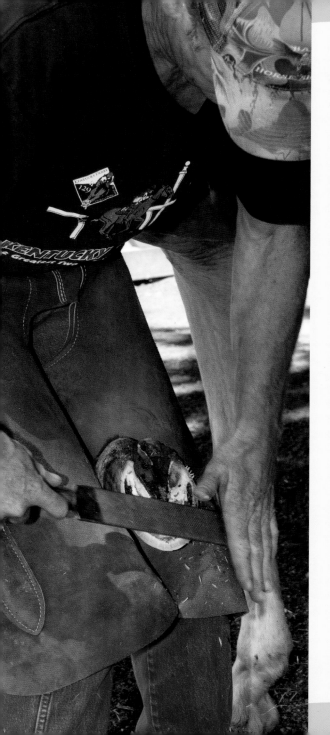

Horse's hooves must be checked regularly by a **farrier**. Farriers trim hooves. They also put metal horseshoes on horses' hooves to keep them from chipping.

Your Horse's Life

With good care, your horse can live well into its 20s. To keep your horse healthy, make sure it gets good food and exercise. As your horse gets older, it may get tired faster. But it will always need your love and attention.

My teeth grow all my life. The vet will make sure my teeth are even and healthy.

Wild Relatives!

Relatives of today's horses were brought to North America by Spanish explorers in the 1500s. Some wild horses still live in North America today. They run free on protected land. These areas are in the western United States and on islands off the East Coast.

Decode Your Horse's Behavior

- Horses put their ears forward when they are interested in something.

- When horses are angry or about to bite, they put their ears back and show the white in their eyes.

- Horses greet their owners and their horse friends with a soft neigh, or nicker.

- Horses swish their tails and stomp their feet on the ground when they are bothered or in pain.

21

Glossary

board (BORD) — to provide care and shelter for an animal for payment

bridle (BRY-duhl) — straps that fit around a horse's head and mouth, used to control it

farrier (FAE-ri-er) — a person who takes care of a horse's hooves

halter (HAWL-tur) — a strap that fits over an animal's nose and behind its ears, used to lead

saddle (SAD-uhl) — a seat used on the back of a horse to carry a rider

stall (STAWL) — the small area of a barn where a horse sleeps

veterinarian (vet-ur-uh-NER-ee-uhn) — a doctor who treats sick or injured animals; veterinarians also help animals stay healthy.

Read More

Bozzo, Linda. *My First Horse.* My First Pet Library from the American Humane Association. Berkeley Heights, N.J.: Enslow, 2007.

Curry, Marion. *Horse and Pony Care.* Horses and Ponies. Milwaukee: Gareth Stevens, 2007.

Draper, Judith. *My First Horse and Pony Care Book.* Boston: Kingfisher, 2006.

Internet Sites

FactHound offers a safe, fun way to find Internet sites related to this book. All of the sites on FactHound have been researched by our staff.

Here's how:

1. Visit *www.facthound.com*

2. Choose your grade level.

3. Type in this book ID **1429612568** for age-appropriate sites. You may also browse subjects by clicking on letters, or by clicking on pictures and words.

4. Click on the **Fetch It** button.

FactHound will fetch the best sites for you!

Index